For my mother

Published by
Princeton Architectural Press
A McEvoy Group company
202 Warren Street
Hudson, New York 12534
Visit our website at www.papress.com

First published in Canada under the title *Je ne suis pas ta maman*
Text and illustrations © 2017 Marianne Dubuc
Translation rights arranged through VeroK Agency, Barcelona, Spain

English edition © 2019 Princeton Architectural Press
All rights reserved
Printed and bound in China
22 21 20 19 4 3 2 1 First edition

ISBN 978-1-61689-760-4

Princeton Architectural Press is a leading publisher in architecture, design,
photography, landscape, and visual culture. We create fine books and stationery
of unsurpassed quality and production values. With more than one thousand
titles published, we find design everywhere and in the most unlikely places.

This book was illustrated using colored pencil and watercolor.

Editor: Nina Pick
Typesetting: Paula Baver

Special thanks to: Janet Behning, Abby Bussel, Benjamin English, Jan Cigliano Hartman,
Susan Hershberg, Kristen Hewitt, Lia Hunt, Valerie Kamen, Jennifer Lippert, Sara McKay,
Parker Menzimer, Eliana Miller, Rob Shaeffer, Wes Seeley, Sara Stemen, Marisa Tesoro,
Paul Wagner, and Joseph Weston of Princeton Architectural Press
—Kevin C. Lippert, publisher

Library of Congress Cataloging-in-Publication Data
available upon request.

marianne dubuc

OTTO
AND PIO

Princeton Architectural Press · New York

In a very old forest there was a very old tree,
bigger than all the others.

In this tree lived a little squirrel named Otto.

One morning, while he was leaving his house,
Otto stumbled upon a strange green ball.
"How odd!" he said to himself. "That wasn't there yesterday."

Otto wasn't too curious. He stepped over the
ball and continued on his way.

A few hours later he came back. The ball was still there.
He went inside without giving it much thought.

The whole afternoon, the ball sat on the branch.

Then, while he was making a cup of warm milk, Otto heard
a noise outside. Oh! The ball had cracked open!

"MOMMY!" cried a creature—very small, very round,
and very furry—from inside the ball.

"No, no, no! I am NOT your mommy!" said the squirrel.
Surely the thing's mother would be coming back.
Otto thought he'd better not get in her way.

Otto wasn't curious, but he was cautious.

Evening came, and still the strange creature
sat inside the green ball, on the branch in the dark.

After a few hours, Otto changed his mind.
"It's fine for tonight, but tomorrow we'll have to find your mother."

"Good night!" said Otto, turning off the light.
"Mommy!" replied the little creature from under the warm blanket.
"No! I am not your mommy. My name is Otto."
"Pio!"
"Alright, Pio will do for now."

The next morning, there was a surprise!
The little creature had grown.
He was three times as big as the day before!
"Pio!"

After gulping down breakfast,
Otto decided to go and ask his neighbors
if they had seen the creature's mother.
"I'm sure she'll come back,
she must be looking for you.
Don't go far, and watch out for the eagle!"
"Pio!" said the creature,
his mouth full of hazelnuts.

Otto went around to his neighbors and told them
the story of the spiny, green ball...

and the little thing that goes "Pio,"

whose mother absolutely needed to be found.

Otto didn't know how to take care of a tiny creature.

But no one had seen the green ball, or the mother
of the green ball, or anything that looked like the small,
furry thing inside the green ball.

Mommy!" cried the creature upon Otto's return.
"I am not your mommy," said Otto. "Tomorrow we'll hang up posters.
I'm sure your real mother is looking for you!"

"Do you want a hazelnut before bed?"

In the morning, Otto woke up to another surprise.
The little creature had grown again.
He wasn't so little anymore!

Otto made posters.
"I need to add some fur. You have lots of fur," he said.
"Pio!" approved the creature between mouthfuls of hazelnuts.

"Stay here and wait for your mommy.
And don't forget—
watch out for the eagle!" said Otto.

While Otto hung the posters on the branches, the furry
creature sat and twiddled his thumbs.

Eventually he decided to make some soup.

"Now, all we need to do is to wait for your mother to come back,"
announced Otto when he got home.
"Pio!" replied the furry thing, offering Otto a bowl of soup.

In spite of everything, it was nice to have such good soup.
"It's delicious. Thanks, Pio."

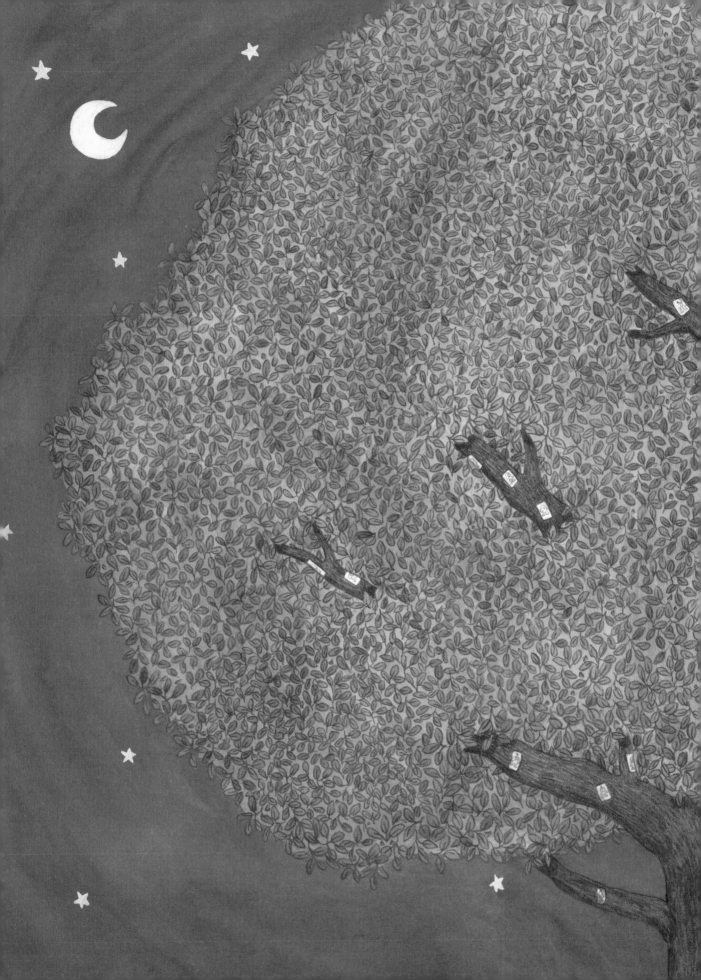

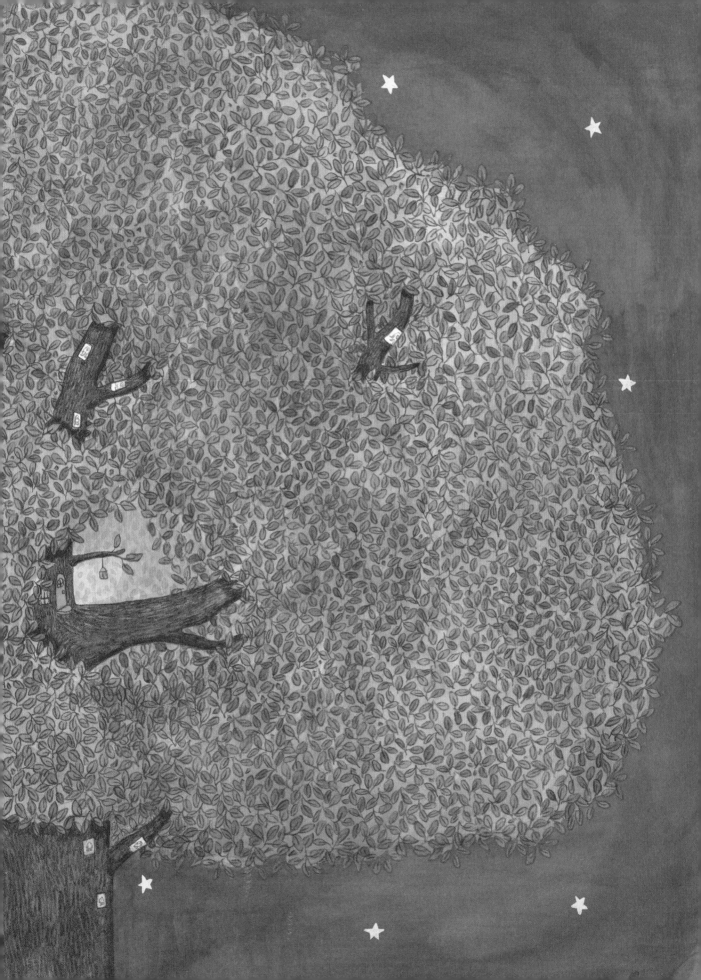

The next morning, Otto woke up to something heavy taking up the entire bed. The creature had grown even bigger!

He was so big that he bumped into everything!
"Be careful where you put your feet!" scolded Otto. "Oh, dear!
We really need to find your mother, and as soon as possible.
You are going to break something!"

Otto decided to go and look in the other trees to see
if he could find some trace of the mother.

The furry creature ate breakfast by himself.
He knew he should stay and wait in case his mother came back.

Otto was gone for several days. He traveled
far through the trees and fields.

He was gone for a long time.
"Pio..." sighed the furry thing.

The wait was endless.

The creature thought that Otto would probably
like to return to a good bowl of soup.

And a clean house.

And maybe some yard decorations.

After several days, as night was falling,
Otto finally came home.

"No luck. We'll have to pick up the search tomorrow," said Otto.
"Pio!" said the creature simply, offering Otto a bowl of hot soup.

The next morning, Otto woke up in a sea of white fur.
Everywhere he looked, there was fur.
The fur of the furry thing. Who had grown.
Again!

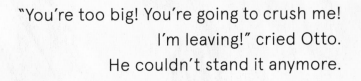

"You're too big! You're going to crush me!
I'm leaving!" cried Otto.
He couldn't stand it anymore.

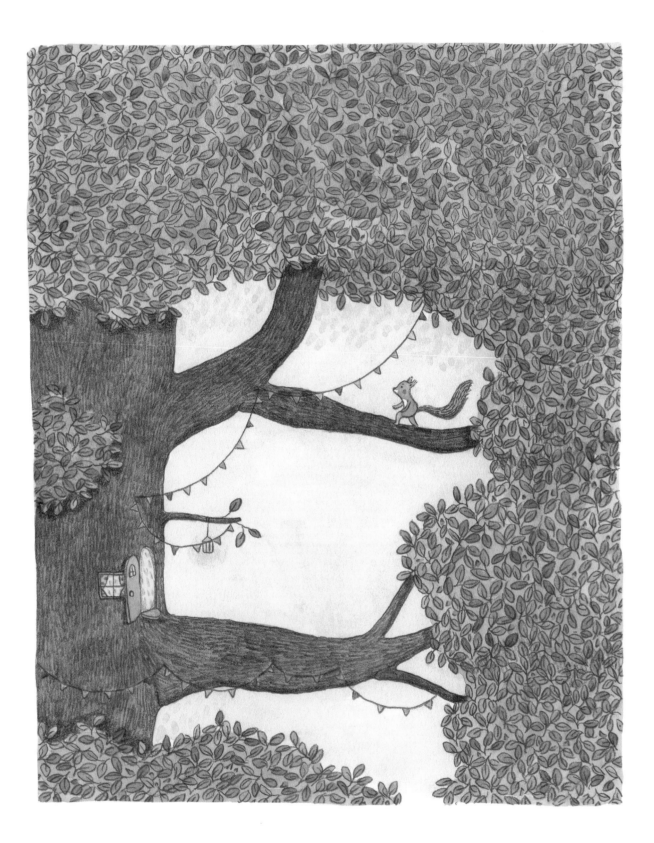

"Whose idea was it to dump a big furry creature at my house?!
I was fine on my own!"

Otto didn't see the eagle circling in the sky.

The forest grew quiet. But Otto didn't notice, he was too annoyed.
"All the same, his soup is so good..."

"And he's nice too..." Otto was thinking.
"And he's not *that* furry. Maybe I just need a bigger house."

Then, suddenly, the eagle dove from the sky, ready
to close its talons around Otto's tail.

Suddenly, there was a piercing

Pio!

The big furry creature ran across the branch,
waving his arms and yelling furiously!

"I'm going home now.
Would you like to come with me?" asked Otto.
"Pio," said the creature, relieved.

"Is there some soup left?"
"Pio!" said the creature.

"I have some house renovations to do.
Would you like to help?"

They never did find the creature's mother,
which was just as well.